Ollie's Halloween

Olivier Dunrea

HOUGHTON MIFFLIN HARCOURT
Boston   New York

To access the read-along audio file, visit
WWW.HMHBOOKS.COM/FREEDOWNLOADS
ACCESS CODE: PROWL

AGES	GRADES	GUIDED READING LEVEL	READING RECOVERY LEVEL	LEXILE® LEVEL
4–6	1	G	11–12	160L

The text of this book is set in Shannon.
The illustrations are pen-and-ink and gouache on 140-pound d'Arches coldpress watercolor paper.

The Library of Congress Cataloging-in-Publication Data is on file.

ISBN: 978-0-544-64054-2 paperback reader
ISBN: 978-0-544-64052-8 paper-over-board reader

Manufactured in China
SCP 10 9 8 7 6 5 4 3 2 1
4500587568

*For the five wee goblins
in my life—
Johnny, Molly, Gabe,
Peedie, and Fergus*

This is Gossie.
She is a wizard.

This is Gertie.
She is a chicken.

This is Peedie.
He is a dragon.

This is BooBoo.
She is a bunny.

This is Ollie.

He is a mummy.

It's Halloween night.
A night to beware.

A night to scare.
Goslings are on the prowl!

Hooting like owls.
Howling like wolves.

Creeping through bogs.
Scaring frogs.

Gossie and Gertie poke
around the pumpkins.

Peedie and BooBoo creep
behind the beehives.

Ollie stalks in the cornfield.

Gossie and Gertie gobble
treats in the haystacks.

Peedie and BooBoo gobble
treats in the cornstalks.

Ollie stares at a ghost in
the open barn door.

"Boo!" shouts Ollie.

It's Halloween night.
A night to beware.

A night to scare.

Hooting! Howling! Haunting!

Goslings bob for apples
in the wooden tub.

In the meadow the scarecrow
shivers in the wind.
Thunder rumbles.

Lightning flashes.
Goslings run back to the barn!

Gossie and Gertie, Peedie
and BooBoo, feast on the
last pile of treats.

Ollie stands
alone in the dark.

It's Halloween night.

A night to share.